Happy Birthday, Sam

Happy Birthday, Sam

by PAT HUTCHINS

 Greenwillow Books

An Imprint of HarperCollinsPublishers

Library of Congress Cataloging-in-Publication Data
Hutchins, Pat (date). Happy birthday, Sam. "Greenwillow Books." Summary: Sam's
birthday brings a solution to several of his problems. ISBN 0-688-10482-7 (pbk.)
[1. Birthdays—Fiction.] I. Title. PZ7.H96165Hap 78-1295 [E]

First paperback edition, 1991
Visit us on the World Wide Web!
www.harperchildrens.com

For Sam

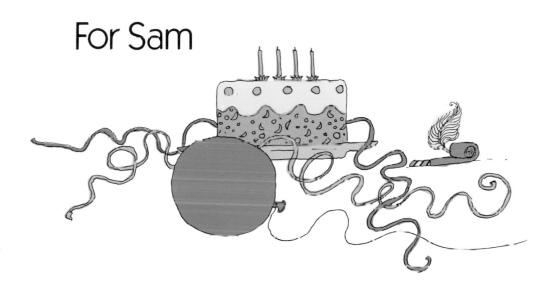

It was Sam's birthday.
He was a whole year older.

He climbed out of bed
to see if he could turn
the light on all by himself,
but he still couldn't reach
the switch.

He went to the wardrobe
to see if he could get
dressed all by himself,
but he still couldn't reach
his clothes.

He ran to the bathroom
to see if he could brush
his teeth all by himself,
but he still couldn't reach
the taps.

So he went downstairs.

"Happy birthday!"
said his mother and father,
and gave Sam a beautiful boat,
but Sam still couldn't reach
the sink to sail it.

"The postman's at the door,"
said Father, but Sam still
couldn't reach the knob
to open it.

"It's from Grandpa!"
   said Mother and Father.
"What a nice little chair,
   and just the right size."

"Yes," said Sam,
  and he took his little chair
  up the stairs,

switched on the light
in his bedroom,

took his clothes
out of the wardrobe
and dressed himself,

and went to the bathroom
and brushed his teeth.

Then he took his little
chair downstairs and sailed
his boat in the sink.
"It's the nicest boat ever,"
he said, "and the nicest
little chair."

And when Grandpa arrived for the birthday party, Sam opened the door and let him in. All by himself.